DARE

Dee Phillips

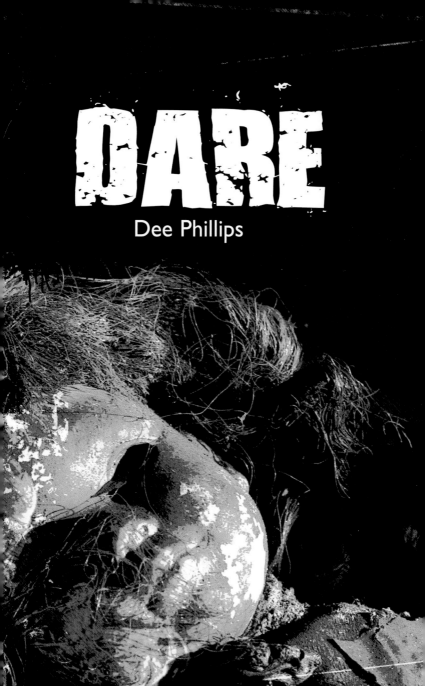

RiGHT NOW!

Blast
Dare
Dumped
Fight
Goal
Grind
Joyride
Scout

First published by Evans Brothers Limited
2A Portman Mansions, Chiltern Street, London W1U 6NR, United Kingdom
Copyright © Ruby Tuesday Books Limited 2009
This edition published under license from Evans Limited
All rights reserved

SADDLEBACK
EDUCATIONAL PUBLISHING
www.sdlback.com

ISBN-13: 978-1-61651-246-0
ISBN-10: 1-61651-246-6

Printed in Guangzhou, China
NOR/0514/CA21400713

18 17 16 15 14   3 4 5 6 7 8

It's just an old, empty house.
I don't believe in ghosts.
That's why I took the dare.

ONE MOMENT CAN CHANGE YOUR LIFE FOREVER

It's dark inside the house.
I shine my flashlight around.
What a place!

OK. I can do this.
It's just a house—an old,
empty house.

I don't believe in ghosts.
That's why I took the dare.

Tonight, I will sleep in this house. Alone.

8

The dare was Kendal and Jasmine's idea.
They don't think I can do it.
Kendal and Jasmine believe in the ghost.
The ghost of the woman who died in this house.

I shine my flashlight
around.
There are lots of rooms.
I try some of the doors,
but they are locked.

Suddenly, I hear a voice.

Please...

I listen. I look behind me.
Nothing.

I shine my flashlight
up the stairs.

Please...
Don't leave me.

The hairs on the back
of my neck stand up.
I'm hearing things.
This old, empty house
is messing with
my head.

13

Upstairs there are more locked doors.

Only one door opens.
I step into the room.
Suddenly, I can't breathe.
My mouth is filled with...

15

...COBWEBS!

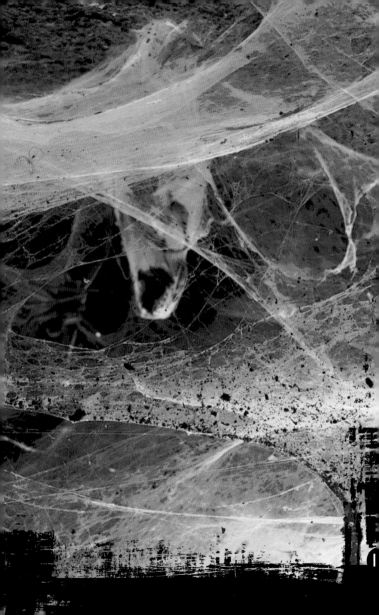

My heart is thump...
I shine my flashlight around the room...
Was this a little girl's bedroom?

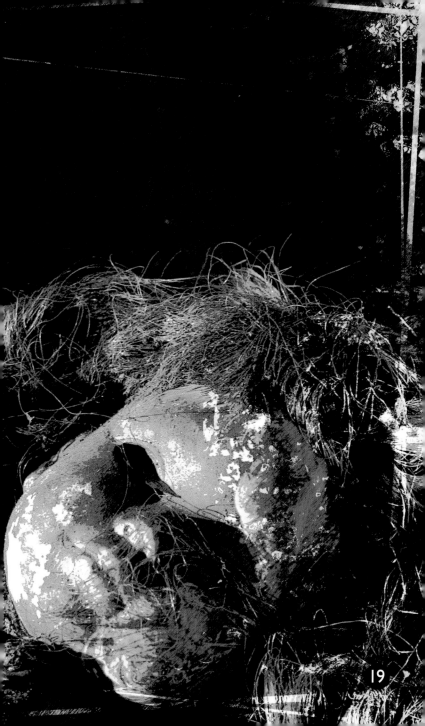

19

Maybe it was a woman's
bedroom?

Then I think of Kendal
and Jasmine's story.

A little girl locked up
by her father.
Locked up in a room
for many, many years.
Then left to die.

There is an old, dusty bed.
I guess I could sleep here.
I put my sleeping bag on
the bed.

I look at my watch.
It's midnight.
I turn off my flashlight
to save the power.

Please...
Don't leave me.
Take me with you.

Am I dreaming?
Is someone there?

I switch on the flashlight.

Yuck!

It's just a rat.

I shiver.
This place is messing
with my head.

I get out of bed.
I can't sleep with a rat!
I have to find another room.

I try to open the door, but...

...it won't open!

28

Is it stuck? Or is it locked?

29

That's when I see the marks.

Marks on the back of
the door.
Is it a hand?

OK. Don't get freaked out.
The door is just stuck.

I get back into my
sleeping bag. It's 3 am.
It will soon be morning.

31

Take me with you.

I'm your friend now...

...forever.

Did I fall asleep again?

I shine my flashlight around the room.
Nothing.
Nobody.

It's 5 am.
It will soon be morning.

35

I wake up and shiver.
It's light outside.

I try the door—
it opens first time!
I did it. It's over.
Now, let's get out
of here!

I open the front door of the house.
The crowd cheers!
I hear the words...

"You did it Kristi. You've won this week's **DARE**."

I see Kendal and Jasmine cheering in the crowd.

DARE is their favorite TV show. Every week, somebody spends the night in a spooky place.

Of course, it's all fake.

A big screen shows my
night in the house.

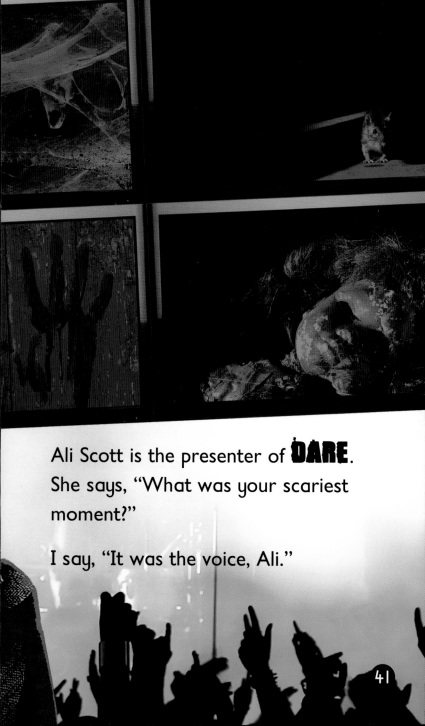

Ali Scott is the presenter of **DARE**.
She says, "What was your scariest
moment?"

I say, "It was the voice, Ali."

42

Ali smiles and nods.
She looks at her notes.
She stops smiling.
She checks her notes again.

Ali says, "Kristi, there
wasn't any voice."

I shiver.

Take me with you.
I'm your friend now...

...forever.

43

HAUNTED HOUSE
ON YOUR OWN

Invent a game based on a night in a haunted house.

- It could be a board game or a computer game.
- You can use events from the DARE story, or your own ideas.

- It could be a board game in which the players solve problems using clues. For example, find a door that isn't locked.
- A computer game could have different levels.

WHAT SCARES YOU?
WITH A PARTNER

Everyone is scared of different things.

- Are you scared of spooky places, such as graveyards? Maybe you have a fear of heights, or snakes? With your partner discuss what scares you.
- What would YOU or your partner do for a dare? Take turns thinking up dares. Be honest about whether you would take the dare or not.

BELIEVERS?
IN A GROUP

Hold a group debate on this subject: *"Ghosts exist in the real world."*

- Everyone decides which side they are on—for or against.
- Each side prepares its argument. Collect as much evidence as you can!
- Hold the debate and take a vote at the end. Which side won?

GHOST STORIES
ON YOUR OWN / WITH A PARTNER / IN A GROUP

Tell a ghost story! It could be based on real events, or make up a story of your own. Make it as creepy as possible. You could:

- Record yourself telling the story.
- Tell your story to a partner.
- Swap stories at a "ghost story" session.

IF YOU ENJOYED
THIS BOOK,
TRY THESE OTHER
RiGHT NOW!
BOOKS.

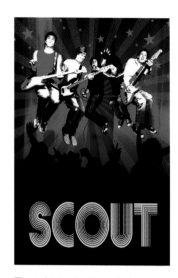

Tonight is the band's big
chance. Tonight, a record
company scout is at their gig!

Tonight, Kayla must make a
choice. Stay in Philadelphia
with her boyfriend Ryan. Or
start a new life in California.

Tanner sees the red car.
The keys are inside. Tanner
says to Jacob, Bailey and
Hannah, "Want to go for
a drive?"

It's Saturday night.
Two angry guys. Two knives.
There's going to be a fight.

Taylor hates this new town.
She misses her friends.
There's nowhere to skate!

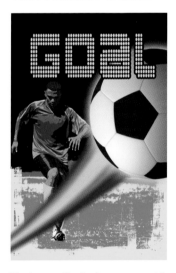

Damien's platoon is under
attack. Another soldier is in
danger. Damien must risk his
own life to save him.

Today is Carlos's tryout with
Chivas. There's just one place
up for grabs. But today,
everything is going wrong!